Written by Emily Gale

Illustrations and cover design by Joëlle Dreidemy

With special thanks to Justine Smith and Hannah Cohen

First published in Great Britain in 2014 by Buster Books,
an imprint of Michael O'Mara Books Limited,
9 Lion Yard, Tremadoc Road, London SW4 7NQ

W www.busterbooks.co.uk

f Buster Children's Books

y @BusterBooks

www.elizaboom.co.uk

A CIP catalogue record for this book is available from the British Library.

ISBN: 978-1-78055-241-5

10 9 8 7 6 5 4 3 2 1

Printed and bound in January 2014 by CPI Group (UK) Ltd, 108 Beddington
Lane, Croydon, CR0 4YY, United Kingdom.

Papers used by Michael O'Mara Books are natural, recyclable products
made from wood grown in sustainable forests. The manufacturing processes
conform to the environmental regulations of the country of origin.

Eliza BOOM'S Diary

My Fizz-Tastic Investigation

BUSTER

TOP SECRET!
↓

THIS DIARY BELONGS TO

Eliza Boom

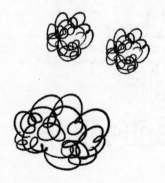

MONDAY MORNING
My Lab, 7am

Dear Edison,

EMERGENCY!

I've lost my guinea pig. I know what you'll say:

> You don't have a guinea pig, Eliza.

My diary, named Edison
(after the famous scientist)

Let me explain. It's all to do with my new invention.

That's me,
Eliza

Lately I've discovered that I can invent
POTIONS as well as GADGETS.

My first potion was for my best friend Amy.

She desperately needed my help.

Amy's mum had washed her hair in mayonnaise after reading on the internet that it kills nits.

Amy wants to smell
like a GIRL ...

... not an EGG!

Result: STINKY!

So I decided to create Egg-Away Shampoo (Potion No. 1) for Amy.

I thought about what girls smell like ...

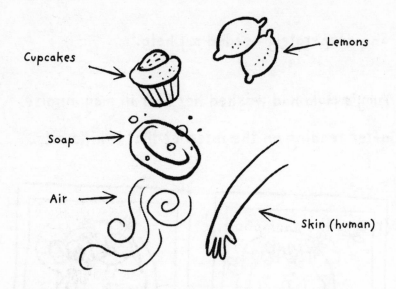

Cupcakes

Lemons

Soap

Air

Skin (human)

... and used all of those things in my potion.

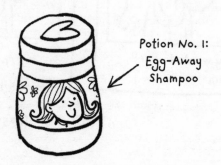

Potion No. 1:
Egg-Away
Shampoo

(Sometimes I smell of dog-hair, too but I
decided not to put any in the potion!)

Finally, we were ready for testing.

Step 1: Saturate test material (wet Amy's hair)

Step 2: Apply substance (rub in the shampoo)

Step 3: Flush excess substance (rinse it all off)

Step 4: Dehydrate test material (dry Amy's hair).

Result: FANTASTIC!

Then I discovered that someone else had a smelly problem.

Alice, my step-mum, was complaining non-stop about Einstein's pong. She's got a nose for trouble. Probably because she's a spy and strange smells are SUSPICIOUS.

Although Dad's a brilliant inventor, he's much too busy to make doggy shampoo. So it was up to me to save the day, and our noses.

Alice, A.K.A. Senior Agent Electra

Plum, baby spy who has potential

Dad, Chief Inventor

Einstein, my furry sidekick

Me, Junior Spy AND Assistant Inventor!!

My family

Einstein and I got to work in my lab. First we needed thinking time. I put on some music to help us relax — I always have my best ideas when I'm relaxed.

The music worked! I knew exactly what should go into the potion. Since Einstein is one of the family, he should smell like all of us!

Potion No. 2: Poochie-Pooh Solution

Ingredients:

1. My toothpaste

2. Dad's shaving cream

3. Plum's nappy-rash cream (only smells nice in the tube, not on her bottom)

4. Alice's face-cream

The mixture was a bit stiff so I added some lemonade.
← Fizz!

It was time for testing. But first I had to ask Einstein a very important question.

Will you be my guinea pig?

Not a **real** guinea pig, of course! Guinea pig is the name you give to someone you're testing an invention on.

I decided to be a guinea pig, too. It was only fair.

I knew Poochie-Pooh was going to be fantastic ... it felt lovely and fizzy on my head. FIZZ-tastic!

The trouble started when we got to 'Step 3: Flush excess substance'. Einstein HATES lots of water.

So that's how I lost my guinea pig. And now I really need to find him.

Yours with fizz-tastic hair,
Eliza Boom
Junior Potions Master

MONDAY AFTERNOON
Our Garden, 4pm

Dear Edison,

I have made a discovery. There's a new neighbour next door and I have **PROOF** that she is mean and horrible.

PROFILE: lady next door
FIRST IMPRESSIONS:
mean, angry
PROBABLY LOOKS LIKE: →

Here's what happened. I followed Einstein's sticky pawprints all around the garden.

While I was hunting for Einstein in the garden,
I heard a lady's voice over the fence.

And I saw Einstein
squeeze underneath.
He looked terrified!

When I tried to get him back inside the house using a brilliant scientific method ...

... he didn't even lick his lips! Our new neighbour had been so horrible she'd put him off his food. Why did she shoo him away? It was a new MYSTERY and I was going to SOLVE IT!

It was a good opportunity to try out one of my latest inventions, The Super-Legs. I used them to peek over the fence.

My Super-Legs Invention:

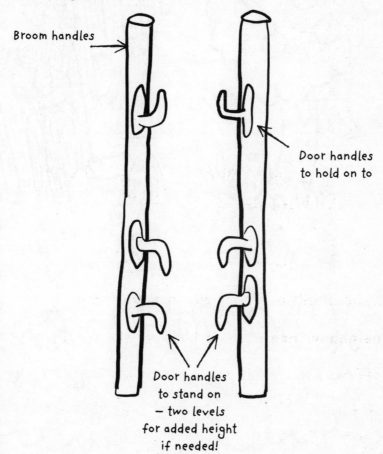

Broom handles

Door handles to hold on to

Door handles to stand on — two levels for added height if needed!

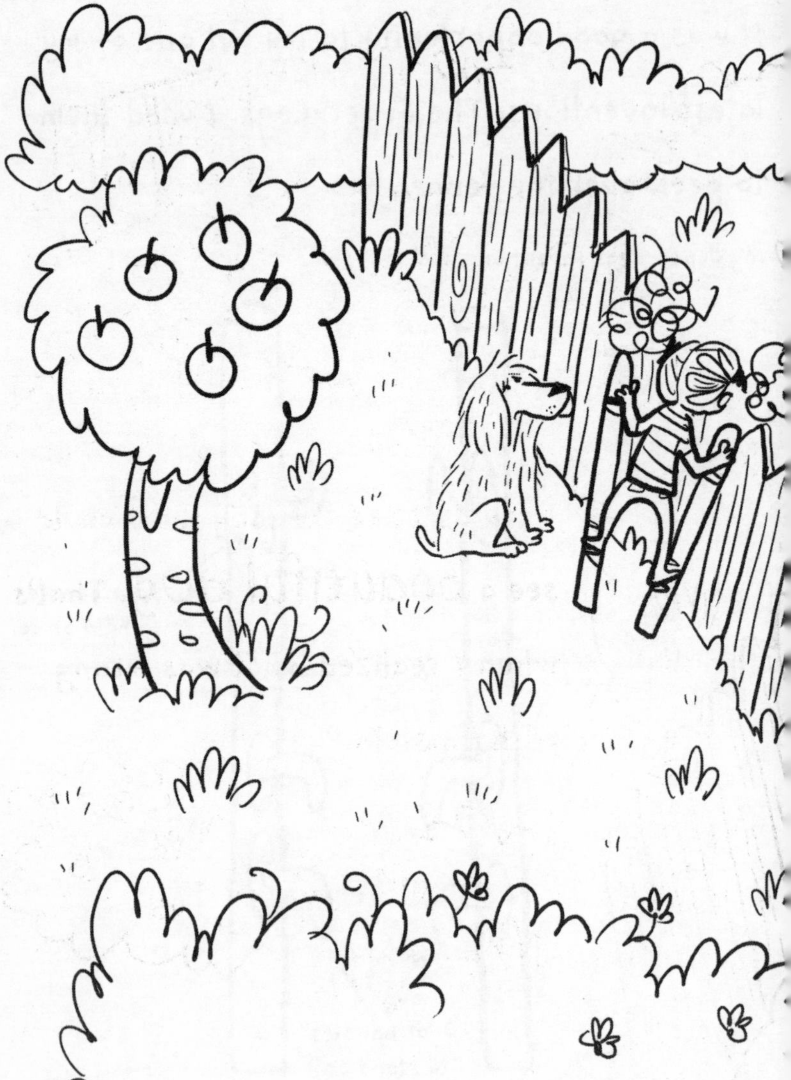

I couldn't see the lady but I could see a **beautiful dog**. That's when I realized what was wrong with Einstein.

He'd found a friend and our horrible neighbour was trying to keep them apart. If anyone tried to keep me away from Amy, I'd be upset, too.

Einstein was so heartbroken he chewed right through one of my Super-Legs!

Yours hopping-mad,
Eliza Boom
Living next-door to an official baddie

MONDAY EVENING
Kitchen Table, 6pm

Dear Edison,

Things just got really weird. The doorbell rang and it was a lady. Not just ANY lady but

THE HORRIBLE LADY FROM NEXT DOOR.

Two things were SUSPICIOUS:

1. She didn't look horrible.

2. She had muffins. And they didn't look horrible either.

They looked ... DELICIOUS.

SUSPICIOUS vs Delicious.

I was confused, Edison.

First, she introduced herself.

Hello, I'm Mrs McNice.

Then, she introduced her muffins.

Hello, we are special dairy-free muffins.

The muffins didn't really speak ... mind you, THAT would be an interesting invention!

Dairy-free, Edison! How could she know I am totally allergic to dairy?

24

Mrs McNice stayed and chatted for a while. When she went to use the toilet, everyone talked about how lovely she seemed.

I decided not to tell anyone that I'd thought Mrs McNice was HORRIBLE before. After all, I've got my reputation as a Junior Spy to protect.

Before she left, I asked Mrs McNice about her beautiful dog.

That's my Nancy. She's terribly shy. I'm so sorry I had to ask your lovely doggy to leave my garden. Nancy was scared of him.

And that's when I had to admit it, Edison.

I had been COMPLETELY WRONG about Mrs McNice.

Yours guiltily,
Eliza Boom
Awesome Junior Spy
99% of the time

Guilty eyes

MONDAY NIGHT
My Lab, 8pm

Dear Edison,

The Boom household is very stressed out.
None of us has had any sleep. It all started
after I finally convinced Einstein to let me rinse
off the Poochie-Pooh Solution.

In return I promised to get him closer to Nancy.

Einstein was whimpering under the hose. He hates water like I hate *swimming*. And I've got a swimming lesson tomorrow. Argh!

What no one seems to realize is ...

... SWIMMING IS SUSPICIOUS.

WHY SWIMMING IS SUSPICIOUS:

1. a) Fingers before swimming ...

→

Before: smooth

b) Fingers after swimming. →

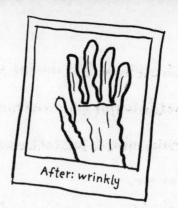

After: wrinkly

2. The drains at the bottom of the pool! Where do they go? And what lives in them?

Swimming pool drain monster

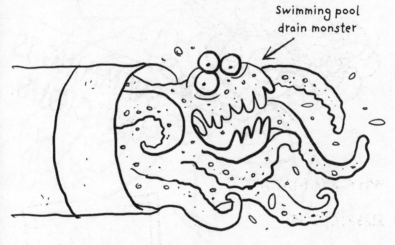

3. Can anyone be REALLY sure that swimming-pool water isn't going into MY PRECIOUS BRAIN?

So I decided to invent something to help me get through my swimming lesson, ALIVE.

I was about to start work when Alice called out for me.

ELIZA!

I was super-excited: maybe she had a new spy job for us!

But it wasn't a spy job at all.

It was a Plum job.

Her night-light was nowhere to be seen.

Plum can't sleep without
her night-light.

Plum's
night-light

Alice was in despair. And all eyes were on
Einstein. Even mine. He has a habit of burying
things in secret stashes — often under the bed
or in the garden.

But spying on Einstein to see where he'd hidden the night-light would have to wait. First I had to use music to get Plum to sleep ...

Plum's room

... so I could stay in my lab and keep working on my swimming lesson invention. My lesson was in less than 11 hours. Argh!

My room

Yours inventively,
Eliza Boom
Super-Spy/Super-Bad Swimmer

TUESDAY MORNING
The Bathroom, 8am

Dear Edison,

My swimming lesson is in one hour.

Scared eyes

But I've decided to face my fears ... with lots of safety equipment.

My new Learn-Away Swim-A-Fish invention is brilliant, even if I do say so myself.

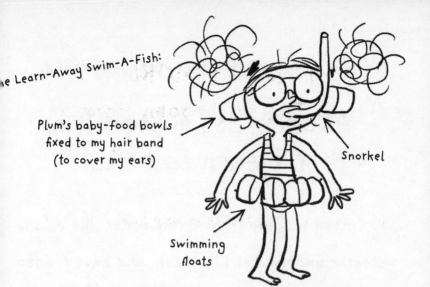

The Learn-Away Swim-A-Fish:

Plum's baby-food bowls
fixed to my hair band
(to cover my ears)

Snorkel

Swimming
floats

Dad said something last night that he hoped
might make me feel better.

Eliza, as soon as you
learn to swim you'll be
just like a fish.

But I think he got that the wrong way round.

As soon as I'm like a fish, I'll learn to swim.

So I need to glide through the water like a fish, breathe underwater like a fish, and have hidden ears ... like a fish!

Me, in fish form, swimming brilliantly

Alice has just finished a bubble bath, so now I can use the water for testing my invention.

Stand back, Edison

— I'm going in!

Dear Edison,

We're buckled-up in the car and ready to head to the pool.

Testing went as well as it could. It's not easy to swim in a bath, and I couldn't see because of all the bubbles.

I've just seen Mrs McNice carrying **four HUGE** planks of wood.

What would she be doing with those?

Hang on, I'm going to ask Alice if this is **SUSPICIOUS**.

Suspicious eyes

39

Oh well, Alice says it is **not** suspicious.

I asked her if she was sure. She said
definitely.

I asked her again. She said absolutely.

I asked her again. She said

ELIZA! PLEASE!

We're moving now, Edison. I'd better stop

because I can hardly read my writing!

40

TUESDAY AFTERNOON
My Lab, 3pm

Dear Edison,

I know you want to know how my swimming lesson went.

But I don't want to talk about it. Ever.

So I'll draw it.

1.

Zoe Wakefield — Class
Meanie/Mean Amphibian
(i.e. mean on land
AND water)

2.

3.

4.

I knew swimming was SUSPICIOUS!

That's loads of suspicious things! I decided to make a Suspicious List:

THINGS I FIND SUSPICIOUS:

1. Zoe Wakefield (why so mean?)

2. Yoghurt (smells like trouble)

3. Mrs McNice (shouty one minute, brings muffins the next ... and why does she need those huge planks of wood??!)

4. Swimming (how other kids can do it is a MYSTERY)

I haven't got time to mope around. I need to hunt down where Einstein has buried Plum's night-light. But I'm going to need an invention ...

I've got an idea! This time, I've been inspired by bats because they are such great **HUNTERS**.

Check out my new Echo-Detector invention:

A head torch: bats have amazing eyesight in the dark

A kazoo: bats make noise to help them find their prey

Big ears made out of papier-mâché painted black: bats have super hearing

Wings made out of black bin-liners: wings just for decoration (but I wish I could fly!)

Bats use sound to hunt down their prey.

So I'm going to use sound to find Einstein's secret stash of all the things that he has stolen.

Einstein is giving me a strange look. Probably feeling guilty.

Strange, guilty eyes

Yours in mission-mode,
Eliza Boom
A.K.A. Bat-Girl, off to hunt down
Einstein's stash

TUESDAY NIGHT
My Lab, 8pm

Dear Edison,

Things did not go as expected.

Being a bat is harder than it looks. I hunted like
a bat all over the garden and found ...

... NOTHING!

When I stopped, however, I **did** hear a
suspicious noise.

Buzz Fizz

It was coming from Mrs McNice's house.

First the ENORMOUS planks of wood,
and now a strange FIZZY-BUZZY sound.

What could be going on in there? Edison,
is it possible I was right? Is Mrs McNice
SUSPICIOUS after all?

Friendly

Suspicious

I really need Alice to train me properly on how to be a good spy, but she's too busy trying to get Plum to sleep without the night-light. It's getting late. I'll have to decide about Mrs McNice tomorrow.

Night-night, mind the bats don't bite.

Yours suspiciously,
Eliza Boom
Assistant Inventor Junior Spy, who will never swim like a fish, or hunt like a bat, ever!

WEDNESDAY MORNING
Our Garden, 11am

Dear Edison,

I'm at my new outdoor lab (it's also the garden bench). Amy's here, too. She's come to help me.

Earlier, Dad was locked in his shed and Alice was in her spy bunker underneath the garden, busy doing top-secret things.

So we were in charge of Plum.

I had thought of a way to spy on Mrs McNice
AND get Einstein closer to Nancy
... another potion!

My plan was to
cover Einstein in a
perfume that would
make him irresistible
to lady dogs.

Then we'd go to Mrs McNice's house. While the dogs got to know each other, I'd find out what that strange fizzy-buzzy noise was.

Some possible explanations for the
fizzy-buzzy sound are:

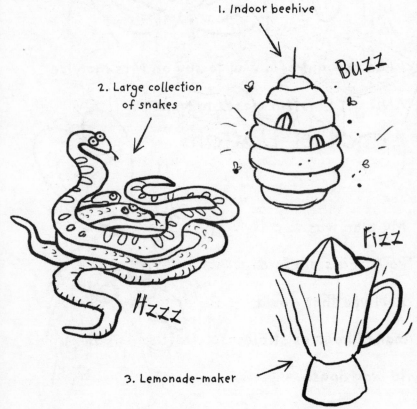

1. Indoor beehive

Buzz

2. Large collection of snakes

Hzzz

Fizz

3. Lemonade-maker

Potion No. 3: Lovey-Dovey-Doggy →

was easy to make.

Plum picked petals from the rose

bush that grows on top of our secret

spy bunker.

We mixed petals with sugar and fizzy water.

Alice says fizzy water is for special occasions

and this was one of those: Einstein's feelings

for Nancy are real.

We dabbed the potion behind Einstein's ears
and did a sniff-test.

He needed a bit more ... and a bit more ...

Result:
He looked like a wet
rose bush. But he
smelled great!

Unfortunately, Plum started playing copy-cat ...
or rather, copy-dog and ...

... splashed the potion everywhere. Poor Einstein got soaked and ran away again!

Where could he be? *Is he with Nancy at Mrs McNice's house?* This calls for a new spy invention. Amy had to go but now *I'm* back in my lab, Edison, making my next invention.

Yours stickily,
Eliza Boom
Inventor, Spy (and missing her furry sidekick)

WEDNESDAY NIGHT
My Lab, 8pm

Dear Edison,

Meet my new invention: The Magni-Visor.

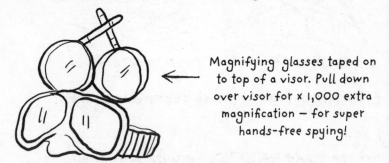

Magnifying glasses taped on to top of a visor. Pull down over visor for x 1,000 extra magnification — for super hands-free spying!

It is very reliable, **UNLIKE** the rest of today, which was very **SUSPICIOUS**.

With the Magni-Visor in place, I crept along to Plum's bedroom window to get a good view of Mrs McNice's living-room. I had to see if Einstein was there.

56

But when I took my first peek, this is what I saw:

Mrs McNice looking right back at me!

When I plucked up the courage to look again,
she'd vanished.

I stayed watching for ages with my spy notepad ...

Here's what my pad looked like after two hours:

2pm No movement

2.30pm Still nothing

3pm Fly lands on
windowsill

3.05pm Fly flies away

4pm I miss that fly

And then came the most difficult test of my spy abilities ...

... I could smell baking! The smell was so good that real tears came into my eyes.

Hungry eyes

But I couldn't possibly move! Spies cannot just leave their position. It's the first rule of a stake-out.

At last, there was something to look at.

I saw Alice and Plum, with a tray of cupcakes (that's what I could smell!), walking up Mrs McNice's front path.

Was Alice giving Mrs McNice cupcakes just to be nice? OR had she become SUSPICIOUS about her like me?

We needed a family spy meeting A.S.A.P.

Just then Einstein came running in, howling.

He was covered in ants!

Poor thing. Instead of making Nancy fall in love

with him, I'd made ants fall in love with the

sticky potion that was all over his fur!

With only one Super-Leg left, I had to use the boring old bench to spy over the fence again. What was going on in there with Mrs McNice and Alice and Plum and the cupcakes?

I hosed off Einstein at the same time. He was being so brave. Suddenly, I saw something strange.

I spied Nancy, the lady dog, sitting beside a table. **HERE IS THE SUSPICIOUS PART** ...

... Nancy was right next to the cupcakes but she wasn't even sniffing them! If Einstein saw those cupcakes, this is what would happen:

Before

After

I ran to get my Magni-Visor for a better look out of Plum's bedroom window.

When Alice got home she asked me why she could see me spying on Mrs McNice's house.

I was honest, of course.

I said I had seen and heard SUSPICIOUS things.

And guess what? Alice told me off!

How can a spy tell off another spy for spying?

Well, Edison, I'll tell you how.

Eliza, would you spy on your friend Amy? Because Mrs McNice is my friend, you know!

So I guess a family spy meeting is out. After all, if the Senior Spy (Alice) doesn't think Mrs McNice is SUSPICIOUS, why should the Junior Spy (me)?

But I can hear that strange **FIZZY-BUZZY** sound right now.

Even with my big ears on, I still can't work out what is making the noise

I'm going to try to sleep.

Most likely I'll just lie awake thinking about more things that could make that strange FIZZY-BUZZY sound.

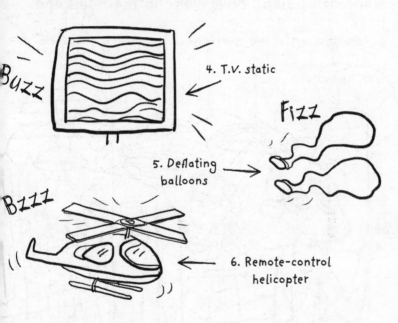

Buzz

4. T.V. static

Fizz

5. Deflating balloons

Bzzz

6. Remote-control helicopter

Yours fizzy-buzzingly,
Eliza Boom
The only spy in the house who feels
SUSPICIOUS!

THURSDAY MORNING
My Lab, 9am

Dear Edison,

None of us slept. Plum woke in the night and screamed until we switched on every light in the house.

I had to invent a soundproof bat cave to sleep in.

Poor Plum still misses her night-light and everyone still blames Einstein. We need that night-light!

So this morning I went outside to look for clues.

Something was different. There was less sky on one side!

Before

After

Mrs McNice had used the huge planks of wood to make her fence taller.

I couldn't even see over it anymore!

70

We stayed out in the garden for a while. I tried to look for the night-light AND more clues about Mrs McNice, but I kept getting confused about what I was looking for ...

This could be a clue. For something. I'm just not sure WHAT!

The hardest part was that Einstein refused to walk on the grass. After what happened on Wednesday, he's terrified of ants.

When we came back inside, Alice said:

You've just missed Mrs McNice. She popped in for coffee.

I couldn't believe I'd missed my chance to interrogate ... um, I mean "politely ask" Mrs McNice about the new fence. I inspected where she'd been for clues instead.

Exhibit A: milk and two sugars

I was adding more to my Suspicious List ...

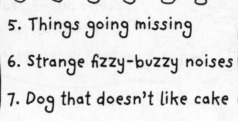

5. Things going missing

6. Strange fizzy-buzzy noises

7. Dog that doesn't like cake

... when clever Einstein found me another clue!

A remote-control
that I'd never
seen before. ↓

I've hidden the mystery remote-control in my lab.
I've also decided not to tell Alice or Dad about
my list until I've got some proof.

Anyway, what if I'm still wrong about Mrs McNice? I don't want Dad and Alice thinking I'm a rubbish spy. I'll have to work solo.

Sometimes it's hard being an Assistant Inventor, a Junior Spy AND a normal kid. For example, right now I'm off to gymnastics class. Spies need to be super-fit and able to leap between buildings.

Yours cart-wheelingly,
Eliza Boom
Wheeeeeeeeee!!

THURSDAY EVENING
My Lab, 6pm

Dear Edison,

As we were leaving for gymnastics, I saw the
MOST SUSPICIOUS THING YET:

Mrs McNice was throwing away the cupcakes

that Alice made for her!

I didn't tell Alice in case
it hurt her feelings.

But that has got to be
SUSPICIOUS

hasn't it? Perfectly

yummy cake in the bin!

Gymnastics class gave me a good idea for how to keep an eye on Mrs McNice:

I needed to invent something to help me jump super-high so I could see over that fence. I used the Super-Leg that Einstein didn't chew through to create ...

... The Super-Leg Boing-Master!

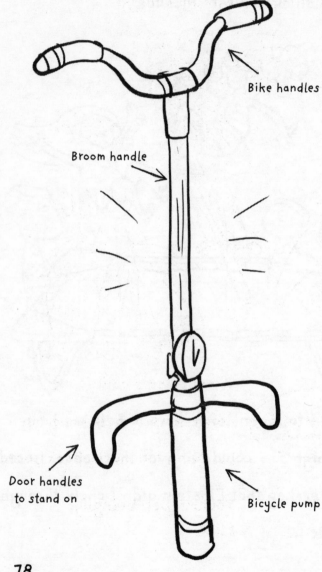

Bike handles

Broom handle

Door handles
to stand on

Bicycle pump

I've been practising up here in my lab. It's brilliant — I can touch the ceiling!

BOING!

BOING!

BOING!

Eliza!

Uh-oh, Dad's calling me downstairs. I must have been boinging too much. Back soon!

Yours super-boingily,
Eliza

THURSDAY NIGHT
My Lab, 8pm

Dear Edison,

You won't believe it but even more things have gone missing!

And guess who everyone **Still** thinks is to blame?

Alice is missing her spy-belt. It's got loads of great gadgets on it — like a micro-earlight, a motion alarm and a micro-listener. Dad made it for her for their wedding anniversary last year.

Einstein would never take it! Would he??

And Dad is missing his spy-pen. Not only does it write in invisible ink but it can also make videos, record your voice, connect to the internet, talk AND even read your mood.

YOU ARE FEELING: INVENTIVE!

It was Dad's latest invention and all his new ideas are stored on it.

But Einstein is INNOCENT. He wouldn't bury them. Those objects are just lost in our house.

Dad says that losing that pen feels like losing a piece of himself.

But which piece?

Brain?

→ Zombie Dad

Heart?

→ Mean Dad

Big toe??

→ Hopping Dad

It's time to think.

Edison, I've got it!

The one thing all of the missing items have in common is:

night-light —→
spy-pen —→ **METAL**
spy-belt —→

YES! All I need is a brilliant invention that uses
MAGNETS!

The trouble is, I need something from Dad's shed, but it's all locked up for the night.

Dad's shed

Oh, Edison, how will I sleep with this exciting idea fizzing around in my head?

Yours, fizz-buzzingly,
Eliza Boom
Junior Inventor with trusted (I think!)
sidekick Einstein

FRIDAY MORNING
The Kitchen, 10am

Dear Edison,

I was up super-early and snuck down to Dad's shed with Einstein.

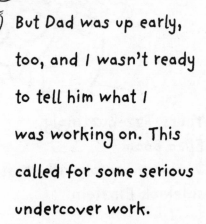

But Dad was up early, too, and I wasn't ready to tell him what I was working on. This called for some serious undercover work.

Luckily for me, Dad was working on his Virtual
Reality Mask 2000.

He couldn't see us even when we were right in
front of him!

I got what I needed from Dad's shed.

Before going back to the lab, I tested out my Super-Leg Boing-Master to see over Mrs McNice's new fence.

But all I could see was Nancy. She was sitting very still in her usual position.

Hmm, Edison, I don't think Einstein and Nancy are a good match. Einstein is lively and fun. Nancy is like a statue!

After some super-high hopping, it was back to the lab.

Dad is always saying that recycling is important. So he'll probably be happy to find out that I've recycled his first-ever invention.

U-bend of a sink

Broom handle

Satchel for storing bounty (treasure)

Compass

Frisbee that works as a metal detector (clever Dad!)

Boom's Bounty-Tracker

He made it when he was my age.

It was obvious that Dad had used a lot of things
from around his house to make it. I bet Gran
and Grandad had a few things to say about that!

That's why I knew Dad would understand
why I HAD to use his Bounty-Tracker in my
new invention ...

I have combined the main parts of Dad's Bounty-Tracker with my Echo-Detector to make ... The Echo-Metal Bounty-Detector.

Let's call it the E.M.B.D. because it takes AGES to write its full name. With the hunting powers of my Echo-Detector + the metal-tracking powers of Dad's Bounty-Tracker, I'll find those objects in the house in no time and prove Einstein's innocence!

Unfortunately the accused dog, A.K.A. Einstein, didn't want to come — he'd been looking out of the window at Nancy since we got up.

Come on, Einstein!

So it was a solo mission to find Plum's night-light, Dad's spy-pen and Alice's spy-belt.

WANTED

DEAD OR ALIVE

I went into every room in the house and piled up the things the E.M.B.D. found in my Secret Spy Stockroom (A.K.A. Plum's room), so that I wouldn't find the same thing twice.

Secret Spy Stockroom

This is what I ended up with:

The good news:

The E.M.B.D. works! I found every single metal object in our house.

The bad news:

I didn't find the spy-belt, the pen or the night-light.

And now I've got to put all the stuff back.

I hope I can remember where everything goes!

Yours, still confused,
Eliza Boom
Assistant Inventor, Junior Spy and about to be in big trouble if I don't tidy up this mess!

FRIDAY NIGHT
My Lab, 8pm

Dear Edison,

I'm going to confess something that I've never confessed before.

I've run out of ideas!

HELLOOOOOOO??

Don't tell ANYONE.

I've been walking around the house all afternoon pressing the buttons on this mysterious remote-control that Einstein found yesterday.

It doesn't seem to do anything.

Alice and Dad have been up to say goodnight.

They said Nancy has been barking all day. Now they mention it, I guess she has ...

I wonder if she's pining for Einstein the way he's pining for her.

I'm going to sleep with the remote-control under my pillow. Maybe then an idea will come to me in my sleep about what it's actually for.

Bark

Yours, puzzled,
Eliza Boom
ONCE an Assistant Inventor and Junior Spy who NEVER ran out of ideas ...

P.S. I wish Nancy would stop barking so much!

SATURDAY MORNING
The Garden, 9am

Dear Edison,

We didn't get much sleep AGAIN.

There was Plum screaming her head off because of the dark.

AND Nancy didn't stop barking all night!

I got up to find Einstein guzzling
Lovey-Dovey-Doggy.

Einstein! You're not supposed to DRINK IT.

Buuurrrrrrrp!

And that's when it struck me: all our problems
had begun the day Einstein met Nancy.

So it was time to retrace his steps.

I didn't know what I'd need for this mission so I grabbed all the spy kit I could carry.

Plum wanted to come, too. And Einstein was so excited about seeing Nancy again he forgot all about his fear of ants in the grass. That's real love.

We arrived at the spot where I'd first seen

Einstein squeezing under Mrs McNice's fence.

I started to dig. Einstein kept watch.

Suddenly I hit something hard and my E.M.D.B. started going crazy. It had to be something metal. And soon I had uncovered ...

Plum's night-light!

Plum was so happy, she hugged it and toddled off into the house to show Alice.

Awww

So naughty Einstein **DID** take the night-light after all.

But the spy-belt and spy-pen were STILL
nowhere to be seen.

That's when I hit something else ... an idea.
What if there were TWO thieves at work?

If Einstein liked to take things and bury them,
maybe Nancy did, too!

First I tried boinging
over the fence.

That didn't work.

Then I tried
digging under
the fence.

That didn't
work either.

Finally, I decided to go THROUGH the fence!

Okay — THAT didn't work either.

Edison, there's only one thing for it: we'll have to ring Mrs McNice's doorbell and use clever spy tactics. WATCH THIS SPACE.

Yours intrepidly,
Eliza Boom (with a bruised bottom)

SATURDAY NIGHT
My Lab, 8pm

Dear Edison,

You won't believe what's happened. I can still feel the shock fizzing in my veins!

Before heading over to Mrs McNice's house, I decided to drop my E.M.D.B. and the Super-Leg-Boing-Master back at our house. As Einstein and I were leaving, I saw Plum playing with that strange remote-control.

I decided to take it with me.

Nancy was barking like mad AGAIN. Was she trying to tell us something? Dogs on T.V. are always doing that.

I rang Mrs McNice's doorbell and quickly hid.

Einstein played his part perfectly.

First he sat there. Then ... he stayed sitting there. Then ... he sat a bit more.

Then, he picked up Mrs McNice's door mat and she chased him all down the street!

I slipped inside the house. I had to work fast ...

Nancy was sitting on a very strange platform. Up close, I could see there was something wrong. Or rather, I could SNIFF it. Nancy didn't smell like a dog, she smelled like ... like a new toy!

In surprise I dropped the remote-control. And when it landed, Nancy barked!

So I picked it up and pressed one of the buttons. Every time I did, Nancy barked.

NANCY WAS A ROBOT DOG!

Suddenly, there was a noise behind me.

Mrs McNice was back from chasing Einstein
and she didn't look like the kind lady who
had brought us muffins anymore. She looked
triple-suspicious.

I tried to be super-brave.

YOUR DOG IS A ROBOT, Mrs McNice!

She didn't look one bit surprised. She looked angry. She started a strange karate-dance.

What are you doing here? Stand back! I am highly dangerous!

Just at that moment, Einstein came rushing
in trying to lick Mrs McNice's face. He was
protecting me, Edison! With doggy slobber.
Good spy-dog!

Panicking, I pressed the remote control.
Nancy darted forward and sent Mrs McNice
flying through the air! She landed — SPLAT
— against the wall.

She must have landed right on a switch, because a huge painting started to move completely **by itself!** Behind the painting was a **Secret room** that looked just like Alice's secret spy bunker.

Fizz

So many machines, all **fizzing** and
buzzing away ... and screens that all
showed different rooms in **OUR HOUSE.**

Mrs McNice had been spying! On **US.**

Buzz
Fzzz
Fizz
Bzzzz

Dad's
spy-pen

And then I saw Dad and
Alice's missing things!

Alice's
spy-belt

At that moment Mrs McNice chased me out of the secret room. Thinking fast, I ran behind Nancy and kept pressing the buttons on the remote-control, keeping Nancy as a guard-dog between me and Mrs McNice. Einstein was helping in his own way, licking her every time she tried to move.

Bark

Bark

Unfortunately, at that very moment Nancy ran out of power ...

... Mrs McNice was coming for me!

NEWSFLASH:

even *spies* get scared.

Scared eyes

Just when I thought I was in big trouble,

and not even my inventions could save me ...

a rescue squad arrived!

STAND BACK,
AGATHA
CREEP!

They were all making a lot of noise.

I have to tell you, Edison, I was confused. Why were they calling Mrs McNice 'Agatha Creep'?

Well, I found out, Edison. That is her real name. And she specializes in stealing enemy plans!

You see, this morning Alice had found my
SUSPICIOUS LIST.

It made her run a check on her digital spy-files.
She found a match! Agatha Creep comes from a
rival spy family. She's been trying to steal
Dad's inventions. (And this time I bet she
wanted my inventions as well!)

Then Alice found five secret cameras hidden
around our house. That's what Mrs McNice must
have been doing when she came round and went
upstairs 'to the loo'!

After a spy conference, we decided not to call the police and to let Mrs McNice/ Agatha Creep go. On **TWO** conditions.

1. She never came back again.

2. We got to keep Nancy. (Einstein will be pleased!)

Dad was relieved to have his spy-pen back. One of the ideas he's stored on it is an invention for me!

Only I have to wait until tomorrow to find out what it is.

What a day! The Boom family is going to sleep well tonight, Edison, **FOR A CHANGE!**

Happy eyes

Yours, still **fizzing** with excitement,
Eliza Boom
Excellent Junior Spy! (Alice and Dad both said so!)
And a really good inventor (they said that, too!)

SUNDAY MORNING
My Lab, 10am

Dear Edison,

six **brilliant** things:

1. Dad's new invention was a special swimming backpack for me. It's made swimming totally non-suspicious and extremely easy-peasy.

2. Einstein and Nancy are best friends.

3. Plum has been sleeping soundly every night.

4. Alice's secret spy bunker is still secret. (Mrs McNice never found it, phew!)

5. Amy and I made lots of Super-Leg Boing-Masters and sold them to our friends. Once we'd done our sums ...

... we had enough money left over to treat ourselves to lemonade!

And finally, brilliant thing number 6:
Zoe Wakefield **REALLY** regrets not buying a Super-Leg Boing-Master.

Fizz-tastic!

Grab your copy of Eliza Boom's first adventure!